DEC - - 2014

For Mr. Will. —M. B.

For C. Schreiber, H. Leatherwood, and N. Beck . . .
the best of the best. —J. C.

Text © 2014 by Mac Barnett.
Illustrations © 2014 by Jen Corace.

Library of Congress Cataloging-in-Publication Data

Barnett, Mac, author.
Telephone / by Mac Barnett ; illustrated by Jen Corace.
pages cm
Summary: In this picture book a string of birds on a telephone wire
play a game of telephone, with the usual mixed up results.
ISBN 978-1-4521-1023-3 (alk. paper)

1. Birds—Juvenile fiction. 2. Communication—Juvenile fiction.
[1. Birds—Fiction. 2. Communication—Fiction.] I. Corace, Jen, illustrator. II. Title.

PZ8.3.B25236Te 2014
813.6—dc23

2013040706

Manufactured in China.

MIX
Paper from
responsible sources
FSC® C104723

Design by Kristine Brogno.
Typeset in Bulletin Typewriter.
The illustrations in this book were rendered in
watercolor, ink, gouache, and pencil on paper.

10 9 8 7 6 5 4 3 2 1

Chronicle Books LLC
680 Second Street
San Francisco, California 94107

Chronicle Books—we see things differently.
Become part of our community at www.chroniclekids.com.

# Telephone

by Mac Barnett    illustrated by Jen Corace

chronicle books · san francisco

Tell Peter: Fly home for dinner.

Tell Peter: Hit pop flies and homers.

Tell Peter:        Prop planes are for fliers.

Tell Peter:
Put your
wet socks
in the
dryer.

Tell Peter: Rock stars are admired.

Tell Peter:
   Crocodiles are bad liars.

Tell Peter: Lobsters are good hiders.

Tell Peter: My monster truck has big tires.

Tell Peter: I'm too high up on this wire!

Tell Peter: There's a **giant monster lobster** named Homer!

He **smells like socks** and he **breathes red fire!**

His eyes blaze like stars and **he rides a crocodile** that flies

and he's coming to this wire!

**Tell Peter to fly!**

**Fly far far away!**

He's too young to be

somebody's dinner!

Hey, Peter.

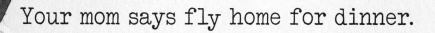
Your mom says fly home for dinner.